Squealer's Adventures

Adam Iler

1ˢᵗ WORLD
PUBLISHING

Squealer's Adventures

Adam Iler

© Adam Iler 2011

Published by 1stWorld Publishing
P.O. Box 2211, Fairfield, Iowa 52556
tel: 641-209-5000 • fax: 866-440-5234
web: www.1stworldpublishing.com

First Edition

LCCN: 2011920346
SoftCover ISBN: 978-1-4218-8602-2
HardCover ISBN: 978-1-4218-8603-9
eBook ISBN: 978-1-4218-8604-6

This material has been written and published solely for educational purposes. The author and the publisher shall have neither liability nor responsibility to any person or entity with respect to any loss, damage or injury caused or alleged to be caused directly or indirectly by the information contained in this book.

The characters and events described in this text are intended to entertain and teach rather than present an exact factual history of real people or events.

I would like to thank everybody that encouraged me to put out my book, So enjoy.

A Pig Lost in Space

Squealer removed some chicken nuggets from the microwave. Before he put the nugget in his mouth, he said, "Better you then me," then shoved a nugget in his mouth. Squealer choked on it and spit it out. The nugget flew across the cockpit and hit a button on the control panel. There was a loud pop and the shuttle lurched. Squealer ran to the window to see one of two fuel tanks floating away. Squealer's heart sunk. With no grappling hooks to reach them and no jet packs to help him fly out and get them, all he could do is watch it drift further from the shuttle.

The remaining nuggets had to be reheated. Squealer quickly punched in the numbers and hit the Start button. Then he went to the console to figure out how he could conserve fuel. Suddenly, sparks began shooting out from the console. Smoke filled the cabin. He turned. The microwave was in flames. "Smokin' barbeque," he yelled, grabbing the fire extinguisher.

Once the fire was out, he opened the microwave. The nuggets were charred. Squealer rubbed ash from the microwave controls. The numbers read "30.35." *I thought I only hit a minute.*

Adam Iler

The electrical fire had cut off all power. Squealer knew there wasn't much time before the oxygen ran out—he just didn't know how much time. So Squealer drifted in his shuttle craft for days. Once he almost got pulled into a black hole. Luckily, he was able to manually fire the last of the fuel in the propulsion rockets. The shuttle broke free.

It was hard for Squealer to ration out the few food packs he had left. "Hmm, vacuum-packed peanut butter and jelly, or mac'n cheese?" he murmured to himself. He decided on the sandwich—leaving the heftier meal for his last.

The shuttle, named "When Pigs Fly," soon drifted near a planet. Sitting at the useless helm, Squealer could see that the shuttle was moving closer, nearer, gravity sucking it into the atmosphere.

"Holy baboon butt!" Squealer freaked out—he knew how hard the impact was going to be. He quickly buckled up and braced himself for a bumpy ride. When Pigs Fly slammed into the terrain with the force of a bomb, shaking the ground. Smoke and debris were flying everywhere.

Dazed, Squealer opened one eye and took a peak around, then crawled out of the seat and stumbled to his feet over to the door. He unhooked the latch to push the door open. The door was a little bent. Squealer took a couple of steps back and threw his shoulder into the door with all his might.

It busted open.

He stood in the doorway, rubbing his shoulder and trying to catch his breath. Peering out, Squealer couldn't see through the thick smoke.

But wait—what the.... Is that just plumes of darker smoke —or—strange shadows—coming towards me....

Squealer collapses.

Waking on Planet Gob

"Uhhhh...," Squealer moaned. His head was pounding. It took a few moments for Squealer's eyes to focus. *Hospital room?* he thought to himself. Someone—or something—was sitting in a chair next to the bed.

"Welcome to Gob," the stranger said.

"Huh?"

"Gob," the stranger repeated. "Don't you know where you are?"

"Not really," Squealer replied. "I..."

"Doesn't matter. Do you know *who* you are?"

"Why, my name is Squealer..."

"Squealer, you say? Well, I'm the Chief of All That Is Creepy, Inc. My people were monitoring your entry into our planet's atmosphere, and could pinpoint where your spacecraft would hit. We were waiting for you when you crashed. How anyone could've survived that is beyond me."

"My shuttle! What happened to it?"

"It's in pretty bad shape," the Chief replied. "My scientists are examining it as we speak. There's a chance they might be able to rebuild it."

"Super!" exclaimed Squealer.

"Sure—now, you've gotten banged up quite a bit, a conk on the noggin, a bunch of bruises, that busted arm, but the doc say you'll heal up fine," continued the Chief. "You've got quite a bit of staying power, kiddo—and smarts too—must have—couldn't fly that bird without some."

"Thanks, Chief." Squealer was more awake now—and feeling hungry. "Say—"

"Yep—strength and brains," the Chief mused. "Now, the way I see it, we have two options. You've entered our space without permission...."

"Now, wait a minute, Chief. I—"

"...so we could put you in prison..."

"Wha-a-a-?"

"...or, you could come work for me."

"U-h-h-h?"

"I could use someone with your talents—plus, all the thugs recognize all my people. They don't know you, so more might end up in the slammer."

Squealer sat in thought. "Chief, how many meals would I get in prison?"

"Three squares a day, kiddo."

"If I worked for you, how many would I get?"

The Chief howled with laughter. "As many as you want!"

On the Job

There are too many, Squealer said to himself, *but I've got to get away from them by using my ray gun.* Squealer tried to reach for his ray gun, but one of the chasers wound up biting him. Squealer let out a grunt and ground his teeth. He had to pull his arm back to get it away from the toothy bucket of bolts.

Why do these little monsters need to have razor-sharp, metal teeth? "Take this, you little over-achieved garbage cans." Squealer grabbed one of the chasers by its arms as it tried to bite him in the face. Squealer lifted it above his head and slammed it down on the ground, making a small crater on the sidewalk. He then took his big round foot and crunched the chaser into a flat disk.

Each of the chaser's arms in remained in each of Squealer's hands. *When are these things going to learn that they will never beat me?* he thought, musing on how his strength has increased since the Chief's scientists devised a special backpack that gave him superpowers. *Good always wins over evil. Everybody knows that.* Then he twirled the chaser's arms like nunchucks, kicking freestyle. He twirled the chaser's arms right into a garbage can and walked away.

Suddenly, Squealer heard rustling among some garbage cans nearby. He thought it was another one of those chasers, so he grabbed his ray gun and snuck over to it. "Come on out of there with your hands up, you sad excuse for a garbage disposal."

Nothing happened. Squealer smirked and said, "Well, then, as much as I don't want to come in there, I guess I have no other choice."

As soon as he began to move forward, a big rat jumps out from behind a box and looks up at him. Squealer threw his hands up over his face, startled.

Adam Iler

Once he calmed down, Squealer said, "Hey, you can't do that to me! I'm a pig—I have a lot of fat on me and it makes me prone to heart attacks. He slapped his belly; it jiggled up and down a few times.

Squealer noticed that the rat had a device attached to its back. He picked it up. "Well, what do we have here?" Squealer asked, with a puzzled look on his face. The device on the rat was pulsating with a lime-green light. Squealer turned the rat around and held it in front of his face. "Are you some kind of tracking device?" The rat just spit out the food that he had in his mouth all over the front of him.

Squealer turned the rat back around. *Roller!* It was Roller's tracking device—he puts his name on everything that he builds. *That's just how arrogant Roller is.* Roller was a robot that wanted to take over this very weird world; he almost did once, before Squealer stepped in and stopped him. *He must've had a bad computer chip when he was younger.*

Squealer took the device off the rat, put the animal down. "There you go, little guy," he said. The rat didn't move, so Squealer took his big round foot and kicked it in its butt. The rat ran away. Squealer laughed. "Well, well, good-for-nothing rodent." He looked at the pulsating device in his hand. *Why would Roller be doing this kind of thing? It's getting harder and harder to find out what Roller is up to.*

Squealer pretended the device was a basketball—he turned around, jumped in the air, and threw the device, aiming for one of the garbage cans. Then Squealer grabbed onto his side like he pulled something. *Man, I gotta stop doing that.* Squealer looked over at the device; it landed right next to one of the garbage cans. *All that work, for what? Nothing,* he thought to himself. He walked away, limping and shaking his head.

Squealer heard a voice—and then felt a poke in his ample waistline. He looked down at a little metal arm with a gloved hand at the end of it, holding out a small TV monitor. The Chief was coming through on his wrist-worn VisCom. "Come in Squealer."

"What's going on, Chief?"

"There's a robot that has been throwing a big tantrum on the south side of town."

"Do you know why?" Squealer asked.

"If I knew, I wouldn't need you now, would I?"

"I guess not....Gee, Chief, I thought you liked me," Squealer said with a teary look.

"Aww, don't get your tail all curled."

Squealer got a stumped look on his face. "But sir, my tail is curled."

"Don't get smart with me, Squealer."

He had a blank look. "I thought I was stating a fact."

"Squealer!" The Chief shouted.

Squealer just looked down. "Sorry, sir. I'm on my way."

"Good luck, Squealer."

"Thanks, sir."

The Chief started to say goodbye, but Squealer interrupted him. "Chief, can I tell you something?"

"What is it, Squealer?" the Chief said with a sigh.

He started to stutter. "Well—I—I—just wanted to tell you to have a great day."

Adam Iler

The chief scrunched up his face. "Thanks, Squealer, you too," he said in a sarcastic tone. "Over and out."

Squealer thought, He's such a cool guy. Well, let me go see what the problem is. So Squealer thought of his little scooter. It burst from the backpack, unfolding as it flew over his head, and slamming right in front of him. Squealer jumped on it and peeled out, heading over to the south side of Grumbles Ville.

The Grumbles Ville Robot

quealer had the speedometer working overtime, buried all the way in the red. He was weaving in and out of people.

"Sorry sir...excuse me ma'am...hey there baby...." *Gee, I wish this thing went faster,* he thought to himself. *But I'm pretty sure it's not the scooter.* He looked down at his belly while it was bouncing in a hypnotizing way.

Squealer flew down one of the side roads onto the main street when a huge foot came whizzing by, almost knocking Squealer off his scooter. He jumped off and skidded across the street, almost running into a streetlight. Squealer ran behind a dumpster. "Could this be the giant robot that is terrorizing the city?" he whispered to himself.

The robot was a steam-powered metal furnace with a fire that you could see in its pot belly and smoke that went through its neck and out of the top of its head. You could see the fire in his belly reflecting off

the metal in the back of his head so his eyes gave off this glow of this dirty orange color.

Squealer got out his video recorder and started a live video feed to show the Chief what this crazed robot was doing. On the live feed the Chief could see the camera pan to the robot and back to the dumpster. Squealer's stomach rumbled in the background.

The robot chased the people on the streets; its stomping feet made craters in the street and sidewalks. Once it started walking over to the dumpster, Squealer started backing away, because he wasn't quite sure what it was going to do. That's when the robot saw him.

"Nice robot—no one's going to hurt you." Squealer waved his hand back and forth, then pointed his finger at the big rusted robot. "Don't do anything stupid."

The robot got mad and started thrashing his arms around.

When he lifted up his huge foot, Squealer saw Roller's stamp on the bottom. "I knew it...I just knew it...I just knew that Roller was behind this," Squealer yelled out loud, throwing his hands in the air.

Now I don't feel bad turning this robot into a barbecue. Squealer got out his ray gun and began firing.

The robot didn't like this to much, so he morphed his arms into big cannons.

"Aw, man! He's got a gun too," Squealer smacked himself on his forehead. "And it's bigger than mine!"

By this time, the only ones on the street were Squealer and the robot—and a little old turtle lady. Squealer said, "Ma'am, could you move? It's sort of dangerous here."

She looked up at Squealer. "Thank you, sonnie, for watching out for me. I don't have anyone to look out for me." She reached into her pocketbook, pulled out some change, and put it into Squealer's hand. Then she shuffled away like nothing was going on around her.

Squealer looked down and opened his hand. In his palm were three quarters, a dime, and a melted chocolate mint.

The robot opened fire on Squealer. Squealer ran from the old lady turtle, taking off down the road so nothing would happen to her. Our hero hid behind a car. Smacking himself on the knee, he thought, *How am I going to take this robot down? Think, Squealer, think.* He peaked over the hood of the car to see where the robot was. Squealer didn't realize that the robot was waiting for him on the other side of the car to pulverize him.

Squealer jumped away from the car in a panic. The robot saw him and took a shot at him, but Squealer rolled out of the way. Every step Squealer took the robot shot huge nuggets of hot fire coal, making craters in the road. One nugget of fire coal flew by him and right into a building, blowing a hole in the wall about the same size as Squealer. Squealer held down his trigger; the longer he held it down the more power shot out of it. His ray gun took off a big chunk of the robot's head. The robot stumbles backwards. Fire rolled out of the robot's eyes and the top of its head.

Squealer thought he had won, but he thought wrong. The robot's arms pulled into his body, turned, and flipped back out. All Squealer could do is shake his head in a daze and wonder what was going to happen. Then the robot started spinning like a top and sparks shot out across the road. These fiery coal nuggets started shooting out of the robot's arms; the sound was like a cannon going off. The coal ripped huge holes in the sides of the buildings. If any more coal hit the buildings, they would start to collapse. One guy poked his head out of one of the building's huge bolt holes asking Squealer what was going on. Squealer looked at the guy like he just fell off the crazy train and told him to get back in the building. "It's a robot that doesn't have all his bolts tight upstairs, if you catch my drift." The guy looked at him and said, "Well, have a nice day."

Squealer dodged the flying coal, hiding behind anything that he could; he even tried behind a telephone pole. *Yah.... A pig trying to hide behind a telephone pole—not going to happen.*

Squealer thought about a big fire-proof catcher's mitt. He started running around catching the fiery coal that the robot was shooting out. "Why do I keep putting myself into these predicaments?" he shouted. "I should be on the black sands of Heli!" The black sands of Heli are on the other side of the planet and that's where the delicacy solar worms are typically found.

Squealer had a big pile of coal nuggets that he collected from the robot. The robot stopped spinning—the firing of the coal nuggets did too. Squealer grabbed his ray gun and opened fire before the robot could do anything else. The robot tried morphing, but Squealer had put way too many holes in it.

Squealer held down the trigger, his power pack beeping to let him know that it was fully charged. Then BOOM... BOOM...He took the robot's head clear off. The robot sparked and twitched.

"Alright—yea!" Squealer jumped, punching a hole in the air. Then he began a jig, dancing all around the robot. The people in the buildings, looking out windows and gaping holes, waved and cheered. Squealer waved back.

He thought about his scooter and it appeared. He jumped on, placed his helmet on his head, and saluted the crowd. "Wherever bad things are happening, just call me and I'll be there." The crowd cheered some more, then Squealer peeled off on his scooter with his hand in the air waving, his tail flapping in the breeze.

Mad Cows

Squealer made a bad choice to call the Chief while he was still on his scooter, using the VisCom on the handlebar. "You should have seen it, Chief. I really clobbered that robot...I creamed him..."

"Squealer..."

"I turned him into..."

"Squealer!" The Chief shouted.

"Sorry, sir."

"That's all right," he said, straightening his neck tie.

"Where are you headed now?"

"I'm headed out of town."

The Chief got a puzzled look on his face. "You mean you're gonna start heading out of town?"

"No, I'm riding out of town right now."

"Why?"

"Goin' to Star Apple Orchard, answered Squealer. "I've got a craving for their apples—watch out, Mr. Cow." Squealer swerved so he wouldn't hit a cow in the middle of the road;

he wound up twenty feet off in a field.

"Squealer, come in...Squealer, come in."

"Yes sir?" His helmet was off to the side on his head; the arm hanging onto the little monitor to the Chief was all bent up.

Squealer sat with a blank look on his face, said, "Squealer over and out," and fell backwards in some broken corn stocks.

The Chief stood up out of his chair. "Squealer, where did you go to?" He sat back down, cupped his chin in his hands, and rolled his eyes. "Over and out."

Squealer had a weird dream while he was knocked out. He dreamt that he was a lot smaller then he is now, but all covered in mud and he liked it. That alone woke him up. He shook his head. *Where am I and what happened?* His scooter was on its side. Looking over to his left, he saw a bunch of cows standing in the field just looking at him. Squealer rubbed his forehead. *Its coming back to me now.* He stood up and stumbled over to the cows. "Is everybody all right?"

One of the cows started toward him angrily, "Let me at him." Another cow held him back.

Squealer looked at him, asking, "What happened?"

"What happened?" the cow screamed out. "What happened? You almost hurt my brother. That's what happened!"

"Then the angry cow's mom started to cry. The cow looked back at Squealer with hatred in his eyes. "See what you went and did? He pushed himself off the other cow and pointing at Squealer said, "You're not worth it. He then walked away.

The cow's mother wiped away her tears. "Just go now." She waved Squealer away. "You did enough here."

He hung his head, feeling as low as the pond scum on the stinky Koukou Lake. "I really didn't mean to hurt him."

The cows turned around and started walking away. Squealer lifted up his head. "I'll make it up to you somehow."

The angry cow stopped, turned toward Squealer, and shook his head. "If you want to really help us, you can find the corn that's missing from the farmer's farm."

So Squealer turned and walked back to the road, mumbling to himself, "There's corn missing from the farmer's farm?"

He jumped on his beat-up scooter to ride back into town. Down the road, the scooter's muffler shot out gray smoke, then backfired, and shot out a chunk of corn cob.

Piggy at Home

Squealer cruised back into Grumbles Ville. He passed the road where he destroyed the robot. The cops and the cleanup crew were making a list of the damages that Squealer and the robot caused; the fire department was also there. One fire truck was putting out a fire out on top of a building, and another was putting out a blazing car fire.

Squealer just shook his head. *Man-o-man, am I gonna hear from the Chief about that one. He just might put me under*

the jail. On his way home Squealer passed the Splash of the Morning, where you can get something to drink and some doughnuts. The only bad thing about the place is that it closes before he wakes up, and that's eleven. *No doughnuts again— and I didn't even get any apples!*

He drove down an alleyway and stopped. He looked around, and mumbled to himself, "The coast is clear." Lifting up one of the garbage cans, Squealer carried it to the other side, then set it down. Part of the wall slid open. Squealer jumped on his scooter and pulled it into his secret place, then the wall slammed behind him.

He rode the scooter down a ramp to his secret lab in the basement. Once he rolled the scooter onto a round platform, he jumped off and went over to a control panel. He hit the repair button. Small mechanical arms rose up from the platform and began fixing his scooter. Along with the arms came a glowing transparent timer that ticked down the time until repairs were complete.

While the repairs were being made, Squealer walked over to his backpack disengage booth. He stepped in, turned around, and slid his backpack into the backpack groove. The machine turned on, lighting up. Its doors closed. A computerized female voice said, "Welcome, Squealer. This will hurt a little bit."

Squealer replied, "It always does." The booth shook and rumbled. He squeezed his eyes shut and gnashed his teeth. Then the machine stopped. The voice came on again. That wasn't too bad now, was it?"

"I wish that I could stick you in this box just one time," Squealer said, pointing his index finger upward to indicate the number one. He walked over to the door and snuck up the inside stairs to the top floor, which was Squealer's apartment. But all the creaking and cracking of those old stairs didn't help Squealer out that much.

You see, Squealer lived up above a Chinese restaurant. The Chief got him this building because the bad guys wouldn't expect a pig to even step near a Chinese restaurant without being on the main course. The restaurant was run by a little spider monkey named Pong. He lives for cooking food, so he's always there. But Mr. Pong isn't the friendly type—he's really mean. He thinks he owns the building, which he doesn't, because the Chief does. Squealer can't tell Pong that—he made a promise to his Chief.

Squealer made it all the way up to his apartment without Pong yelling at him, or so he thought. The door to Pong's restaurant burst open, with a piece of the door frame ripping off. Pong stood in the door with an grimace on his face looking up the stairway. He yelled, "Squealer do you have to stomp up to your apartment? It sounds like a herd of elephants running up the stairs."

Squealer looked over the banister. "Hey there, Mr. Pong, how are you doing?"

"You know that I don't like small talk, Squealer. It takes me away from working in my restaurant. Time is money and the last time I checked you couldn't send your kid to college—if you had one—on how you do things. Just be more quiet—I don't want to tell you again." While he was talking, Squealer was mouthing what Pong was saying. Pong slammed the door shut before Squealer could make any reply.

Squealer mumbled. "Just like the other billion times that you told me. Only if Pong knew the truth." He bent down and lifted up the mat to his apartment, wiping away the centipedes off his key. Opening the door, he threw the key into a wicker basket and   looked at his answering machine. *No messages,* he thought. *I don't know why I even bought this stupid machine.*

He walked over to his pet Betta. "How're you doing, Flip-Flop?" He bent down to get a better look at it, and scrunched his nose up. "I should name you something else, because you don't flip or flop anymore." Squealer reached over and grabbed the fish food, then shook some in the bowl; Flip-Flop swam up, got a flake of food, and hurried back to his castle. He ate his food with shifty eyes.

Squealer went over to his stereo and turned it on. Opera started blasting out of the speakers; he lowered his ears at the music. Then there was a banging under his feet. "Squealer, turn that down—your scaring my customers." Squealer turned it down, then turned the dial to another station. He plugged his head phones in and put them on. *So Pong won't blow a gasket again.* Squealer started dancing around his apartment, dancing over to his refrigerator. He opened the door and rummaged around. "Say, that looks good," he said, "no that looks even better—oh my, I forgot I even had that in here...let me grab some of these...." Squealer stood back up. In his arms there was enough to feed a whole army, or in this case, just Squealer.

He started walking to the kitchen table, then stopped to slam the refrigerator door shut with his foot, and started over to the table again. Squealer laid all the stuff down on the table, looking over everything he put down, which filled up half of the table. Squealer mused, "There's something missing." His eyes got really big. "Bread, he yelled. Bread—that's what I'm missing—bread." He turned around and ran over to the refrigerator when suddenly there was more banging under Squealer.

"Keep it down up there, Squealer," Pong shouted, then banged again.

Squealer yelled back, "Sorry, Mr. Pong," then tip toed over to the refrigerator. He grabbed the bread, turned around, and did a break dance back to the table. Squealer could hear Mr. Pong screaming, so he stopped.

Squealer got his food ready and sat down at the table. It wasn't a pretty sight, and looked as he has never eaten before. There were chunks of food on the table and on the floor and on Squealer's face. He only had one more bite left on his plate. *Man-o-man, I can't eat another bite,* he said, rubbing his belly. He started to get up from the table when he looked back at that last bite of food. It was calling out his name, *Squealer, Squealer,* and he just couldn't take his eyes off it. It was hopeless—he was in a trance. He grabbed the bite off the plate and shoved it in his mouth. Squealer's eyelids sunk down. *That was better than all that other stuff I just ate—a little slice of heaven that I just put in my mouth. UH-o-h-h-h, I think my belly button just went from an innie to an outie.* Squealer leaned back in his chair and started rubbing his belly to get the food to settle down because it was like two lions fighting. "I'm not going to eat another thing for days," he moaned. He heard a noise under him. He looked at the floor like it was going to tell him something. *I wonder what that is?*

Suddenly the legs of the chair gave way and snapped off, the seat to the chair hit the floor, and Squealer landed on top of the seat. It made a crater in the floor. Squealer rolled off the chair, then got to his knees.

He lifted up the seat to the chair, and there in the floor was a view to Mr. Pong's kitchen. Pong had chunks of dry wall on and all around him. Looking up through the hole at Squealer was a very mad monkey.

"Hey there, Mr. Pong—whatchya cooking?" Squealer giggled nervously, giving Pong a little wave. He thought that he could see steam come out of Pong's ears he looked so mad.

One of Pong's eyes started twitching; Pong looked around his kitchen, then looked back up at Squealer. Squealer looked at Pong. "It's not as bad as it looks." Pong got this half grin on his face—"ha, ha, ha"—then let out a big cry.

"Squealer, how could you wreck my kitchen?"

"It was a ...."

Before Squealer could finish his sentence, Pong spoke up, "Accident?"

"Right, Pong, it was."

"There are no accidents when it comes to you."

"Hold on there, Pong..."

"No—you hold on, Squealer. I've had it with your carelessness."

"I'm sorry, Pong."

Pong looked around his kitchen. "Sorry isn't good enough this time." Pong grabbed the dish towel off his shoulder and threw it down on the counter, then turned around. "No, sorry isn't going to do it this time. Pong then walked out of the kitchen, leaving Squealer looking down from the hole, watching the door swing back and forth.

"Where you going, Pong?"

Pong gave no response. He picked up the seat from the chair and looked at it. Squealer let out a big sigh. *It was a accident, though, really it was.* Squealer walked over to his couch and flopped down. One of the springs from the couch shot out and poked him in the butt. Squealer didn't even flinch. He said out loud, "I'm sure Pong ordered that one for me. Read you loud and clear, Pong."

Squealer hit on "on" button of his VisCom remote. *Maybe I can get in my favorite show—I love "Fluffy and Slouch."* The monitor came down from the ceiling and switched on. Squealer settled in and began watching his program. Right in the middle of the show, the Chief's image appeared. "Squealer, come in. Hey there, Squealer—hey, there you are."

Squealer just glanced up at him. The Chief knew something was wrong. "What's going on?"

"I don't want to talk about it."

"Squealer..."

"I don't want to talk about it."

"If you don't tell me, I'll personally make out your new grocery list and just put vegetables and fruit on it for a full year."

Squealer spoke up. "Don't do that! I have to survive off of my food and I can't survive off of fruit and vegetables. I'm a pig—I need fat to live—I need fat to live—can you hear me? The chief spoke up. "Ok, ok, back away from the TV."

Squealer had his hands wrapped around the TV with his nose smashed up against the monitor.

"Now tell me what's going on."

"Well, Pong and me got into a huge fight."

"What about?" the Chief asked.

"Ah-h-h, I sort of put a hole in his ceiling—my floor."

The Chief laughed. "Man-o-man, I couldn't imagine how mad Pong is at you right now. So how did this hole get there?"

"Well..." Squealer hesitated.

"Come on, out with it, Squealer!"

"Well...my chair gave way and I landed on the floor."

The Chief tried to hold in the laughter, but it was like a dam you could only hold back so far. His face got all red. Tears started to form in his eyes, then he tilted back his head and it came out, his shoulders moving up and down as he laughed and pounded on the desk.

Squealer was mortified. "Thanks a lot, Chief. You can stop laughing at any time."

Adam Iler

"Sorry, Squealer." He calmed down. Wiping away some tears, he let out another long drawn out laugh.

In between laughs he told Squealer that he would send a couple of his guys over to Pong's restaurant to fix the hole.

"You'd do that for me?" Squealer asked.

"Sure, that's not a problem."

"How can I pay you back, Chief?"

"Don't worry about it, that story is good enough."

"Oh thank you, sir, thank you."

The Chief just had a big smile on his face. "Over and out."

Squealer started getting up off the floor when the Chief came back on the TV. "I forgot why I got a hold of you in the first place. There's been record numbers on the Richter scale. But what's weird is that it only happens up by the abandoned coal mine.

Squealer spoke up. "But that mine hasn't been active in years!"

"Yes, Squealer, I know. So guess what you get to do?"

"What?"

"You get to check it out!"

Squealer got this scared look on his face. "Do I have to?"

"Yes, you have to, Squealer, and that's an order!...First thing tomorrow night."

"Can't I go in the daytime?"

"No, I don't think so.

"These tremors only happen at night?"

The Chief said, "You can sleep in your bed one more night."

Squealer shouted, "Chief, that's not even funny!"

"Aww, I'm only joking around with you."

"Yea, alright...Should I tell Mr. Pong that your guys are coming by to fix that hole?"

"No, Squealer, I think you should let Pong cool down."

"Yah, your right, and when you're right, your right—and you, Chief, are always right." "Squealer..."

"Yes Chief?"

"Focus, would you?"

"Sorry sir," Squealer said with a big old grin.

The Chief was saying over and out when Squealer interrupted him. The Chief said, "You're really making this a habit, aren't you?"

"I try not to."

"What do you want Squealer?"

"Well, I was going to tell you—" and Squealer blurted it out really fast, "good night and don't let the bed bugs bite."

The Chief just shook his head, then pushed the button to turn off his VisCom monitor.

Squealer got up off the couch and started looking around. "This could be my last night in my apartment," he said to no one in particular. Squealer walked over to his Betta fish. "This could be the last time that I ever see you, Flip-Flop." Flip-Flop just swam to his castle and didn't come out. "Silly little fish," Squealer said to himself. "He doesn't realize what is going on." But what Squealer didn't know is that Flip-Flop was a double agent who worked for Roller. When Flip-Flop swam to his castle, it wasn't to hide from Squealer, but to inform Roller what the Chief had just got done telling Squealer what his next move would be.

He decided to turn in early, so he went to his bathroom to wash up for night. Squealer finished up by brushing his teeth, then gargling with mouthwash. In his bedroom, he had a few posters on his wall and quite a few knickknacks on his dressers and shelves. He climbed in bed. Under the covers of the night Squealer tossed and turned. He just couldn't get this image of a certain pig out of his head. The weird thing about this pig is that she couldn't stand—she was walking around on her hands and feet.

All Squealer could think about is how dirty it was to walk on her feet and he tried everything in his powers to make her stand. After a few tries, this female pig got really nervous. She started running around the cage she was in, when this person showed up and pushed the female pig out into a truck. All Squealer could do is watch it drive off, leaving a trail of dust.

Squealer woke in a panic, shooting up into a sitting position, breathing really hard. His chicken alarm clock was going off. It has a hand around the neck of the chicken; when it says it's time to get up, the hand strangles the chicken and its eyes bulge out of its head.

Man-oh-man, why do I keep having these weird dreams? It's strange that my kind would walk on its hands and feet.

Squealer jumped out of bed and ran to the shower. *A little scrub-scrub there and a little scrub-scrub here, and that's the way we get clean.* After the shower, he ran back into his room and made his bed. Taking out a quarter, he threw it up into the air. It hit the bed and bounced off, of it, hurling back at him and almost hitting him in the face.

Squealer ducked, then he heard some commotion down in Mr. Pong's restaurant. Squealer could hear Pong say something about how he didn't order some guys to fix his restaurant, but "Ok, ok, you guys can come in but don't touch anything." After that, he could hear someone coming up the stairs and pound on the door—any harder and the door would have been knocked down. Squealer said, "I wonder who that could be?" rolling his eyes.

Pong yelled, "Squealer, I know you're in there, open up."

Squealer strolled over to the door. "Who is it?"

"You know who this is!"

Squealer opened the door just when Pong was about to knock again. All Squealer saw is a fist coming at him; he threw his hands over his face. "Don't hit me—don't hit me, Pong!" he screamed out.

Pong, with a disgusted look on his face, said, "I have four men wearing black sunglasses and black suits downstairs in my restaurant and they're here to fix the hole in my ceiling that someone put there—but I won't mention any names right now. The funny thing about the whole situation is, I never called anybody out to look at it. Do you know anything about these guys showing up at my restaurant door—do you, Squealer?"

He wasn't really sure what to say; the Chief told him not to say anything, so all Squealer could say was, "Ah-ah-ah..."

Adam Iler

Mr. Pong got up into Squealer's face. "Well, do you?"

"Pong—I gotta go—" Squealer tried to shut the door, but Mr. Pong put his foot in the doorway, blocking the door from shutting.

Pong let out a whimper. Squealer opened the door back up. Pong barged in, furiously pushing Squealer all the way to the back of his couch and getting inches from his face. "I don't know what you do up here, and frankly, I don't want to know. I run a classy Chinese restaurant and all this noise needs to be cut out."

"There's a lot of noise?" Squealer said with a dumb look on his face, looking from side to side.

"Even after you leave, I still here noise up in this horrible apartment—what's that smell?" Pong waved his hands. "Don't tell me—don't tell me—I don't want to know. It stinks like a barnyard—you have no idea where these guys came from?"

"No way—you think I have that kind of pull?" said Squealer.

Pong backed away, then turned around and went back downstairs. "Just try to keep the noise down, then, will you?" he said, slamming the door behind him.

Squealer slid down to the floor. "Man, does that guy need a vacation or what, Flip-Flop?" he said, looking over at the fish bowl. Flip-Flop just closed his eyes and disappeared in the darkness.

Squealer sat for a while. *Pong said that he heard noise after I left the apartment. I wonder what's going on when I'm not home?* He looked up at his clock. It was only nine thirty.

Squealer's belly began growling—if it was any louder, it

would have shook Squealer across the floor. So he got up off of the couch and went over to the refrigerator. Once he had it opened, he couldn't find much because he had eaten all the good stuff the night before.

Adam Iler

Pig About Town

Then a light came on in Squealer's head. *I could go down to the Splash of the Morning.* So he did. He got dressed, went downstairs, jumped on his scooter, and took off. Cruising down the road, people began recognizing him—first it was little kids, who waved to him, then the adults started waving. Squealer was feeling good about himself, like the job that he was doing was finally paying off.

Squealer turned into the Splash of the Morning parking lot, parked his scooter, locked it up, and walked up to the shop. Little did he know that he was going to meet the biggest goofball ever.

The two clerks in the place—Mandy and Steve—were bored out of their minds. Mandy was a Goth girl, with pale skin, jet black hair, and heavy makeup; Steve, on the other hand, was a class clown who would make anybody laugh. He would do anything to make Mandy laugh, because Steve had a little crush on her.

Mandy was standing there painting her fingernails—you guessed it, black. Meanwhile, Steve was trying to see how many pencils he could stick into the ceiling.

"I've got to find a different job, Steve, if this keeps up."

"You're crazy, Mandy. If they want to pay me to stand here and not do anything, then they're just stupid."

"You just don't get it, do you, Steve? I can think of a million other things I could be doing right now then standing around here!"

"I hear that!" Steve said as he threw another pencil into the ceiling. "Yes! I'm up to ten now!"

Mandy looked up at the pencils and said sarcastically, "Way to go, Steve."

He looked down to get another one when he noticed Squealer entering. "Hey, Mandy," he said, nodded toward Squealer.

Mandy, who was still working on her nails, said, "Did you get another one? Way to go, Steve."

"No—" he said, "look what's coming in!"

Mandy looked up. "You've got to be kidding me."

Steve had his hands on the countertop, jumping up and down. "This is going to be so fun!"

She looked over at him. "What are you going to do?"

"You'll see." Squealer stepped up to the counter and said hi.

Steve spoke up. "How you doing today, sir?" Steve smirked over at Mandy.

"I'm doing great," Squealer said, and looked at Steve's name tag. He said his name out loud, then looked up at him and said, "I'm doing great, Steve." Steve's face turned bright red.

Squealer then turned to Mandy and asked her how she was doing. Steve turned to Mandy and smirked again, laughing under his breath. Little beads of spit were coming out of Steve's mouth. Mandy looked at Steve, rolled her eyes, then looked at Squealer. With impatience in her voice, she said, "Fine, sir."

Steve looked out at Squealer's scooter. "That's a sweet ride you got there, sir." Squealer turned around. Steve pumped his arms back and forth along his sides.

"Yah, it gets me from point A to point B," Squealer replied, then he turned back around.

Steve looked at Squealer and asked, "What can I do you for?"

Steve looked over at Mandy and started smirking again. Squealer thought Steve had a nervous tic, so he paid no mind to it. "Well, Steve, this is my first time here and just looking to see what you have to offer. What kind of muffins do you have?"

Steve stepped over to the muffins. "We've got blueberry, apple cinnamon, apple crumb, banana crumb, banana nut, cinnamon raisin, double chocolate, orange cream, apple and walnut...," Steve smirked on that one, "cranberry muffin, pumpkin muffin, bran, and I think that's about it."

Squealer looked over all of them again, and that's when Steve started to get impatient. His forehead scrunched up.

"There's so many to choose from," Squealer said. Steve just smiled. "What's that one?" Squealer asked.

Steve looked over at it. "That's just our classic muffin."

"Yum—I'll take two of them and a mocha cappuccino to go." Steve got the muffins while Mandy got the cappuccino. Squealer took the money out of his pocket and paid, then leaned in close to Steve. "I know someone who can look at that nervous tic that you have."

Steve's jaw dropped, and Mandy put a hand to her mouth to keep from laughing out loud. Squealer grabbed his stuff, waved goodbye, turned around, and walked out. Mandy started waving goodbye, then saw Steve wasn't waving, so she knocked him in the side with an elbow. Steve then waved goodbye. After Squealer left, Mandy patted Steve on the back. "I guess you don't get the last laugh," she started chuckled.

Holding his side, Steve grabbed one of the pencils off of the counter and threw it across the room. "I guess not."

Squealer put his food and his drink in the food and drink compartment of his scooter; he placed the helmet on his head and took off down the road. Along the way, he drove past the Full Bowl ice cream store, where Stacy worked.

Now, she liked Squealer and he liked her, but he had no time for dating, being a Special Agent and all—plus he can't tell her that he's a agent anyway.

So, when Squealer saw Stacy's little car in the parking lot, he had a hard time convincing himself to turn around and go back to the ice cream store, but he did. He thought the last time that he talked to her she said that they were getting a new flavor of ice cream, cheetah dots. So he pulled into the parking lot of the Full Bowl, parked his scooter next to her car, and went in. All he kept saying to himself is, *Stay cool, I'm just here for some ice cream.*

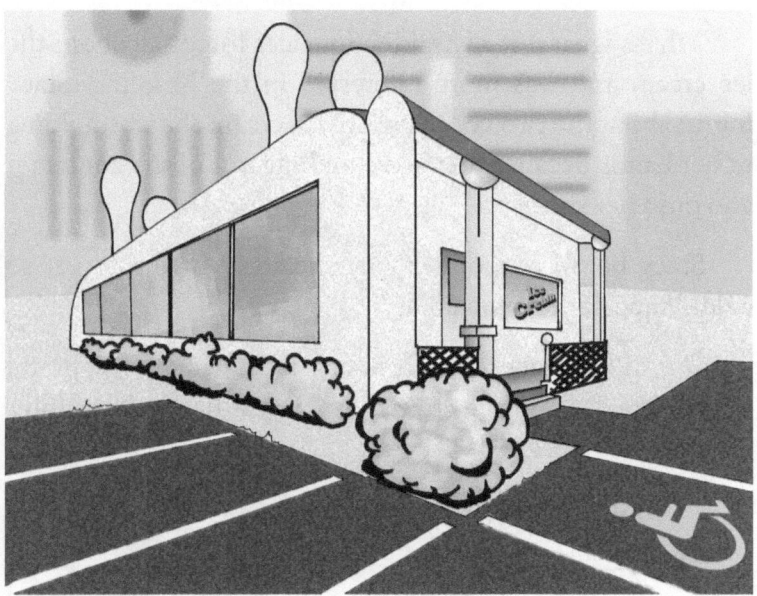

Stacy was in the back grabbing some new containers of ice cream when she hears the bell on the door ring, "Be right with you!"

"Take your time," Squealer's voice crackled, then he quickly repeated it in a deeper voice. Stacy knew right away who it was, so she ran through the curtain with two containers of ice cream in here hands. Then she stood calmly behind the counter. "Hi, Squealer, how are you? Haven't been in here for a while."

Squealer took a step forward. "Yah—I've been pretty busy lately."

"I know, I saw you on the front page of the *Grumbles Times*."

"I was in the newspaper?" he questioned.

"Yah—Local Pig Stops Mad Robot from Destroying Grumbles Ville."

"That's what it really said?" Squealer forgot all about the ice cream and was more interested in the headline. Stacy forgot about the two containers of ice cream she was holding in her hands because they were melting out of the container and onto her shoes.

Stacy began to wonder why she was starting to get so cold. "Squealer, are you cold?"

"No. It feels nice in here because it's starting to get pretty warm outside." And he started looking at her real carefully. "Stacy—"

"Why am I getting so cold?"

"Stacy—"

Her eyes darted around the room.

"Stacy!"

She looked at Squealer. "What do you want?"

"I think I found the problem."

"What is it?"

"Look down."

Stacy looked down and there on her feet was ice cream and a big puddle all around her.

"Oh my...." She looked up at Squealer. "I guess you solved the mystery!" Stacy laughed as she tried to step out of the puddle without tracking it all over the store. "I guess you can't stop what you're doing and start talking with these in your hands!" Then they both laughed.

After cleaning up the mess, Stacy looked over at Squealer and said, "Let me get you something on the house, my treat."

Squealer gave half a grin and asked, "Did that cheetah dots come in yet?"

"I think that's what came in on the truck yesterday, so you're in luck, Squealer."

"Have you tasted it yet?"

"No, not yet, but the truck driver highly recommended it."

Squealer paused. "How does he know?"

Stacy said, "I go on a 'don't ask don't tell' policy."

He asked, "What's that?"

"If I don't ask him, he doesn't tell me!" They chuckled together.

Stacy scooped the cheetah dot ice cream out, while

Squealer looked over the rest of the ice cream. His mouth started to get wet and his eyes glazed over.

"Here's the cheetah dots, Squealer!"

"Thanks, Stacy."

While our hero was enjoying his ice cream, Stacy went back to work, cleaning up the shop before the late afternoon crowd showed up. Once Squealer finished licking his bowl, Stacy said, "Say, Squealer, I've got some refrigeration boxes to move around out back. Could you give me a hand?"

"Sure, Stacy," Squealer said, glad to have an excuse to linger with Stacy.

Suddenly, there's a noise in the back of the shop at the loading dock. They run to the back. When they get there, they see a boy and his robot stealing those refrigeration boxes— full of ice cream. The boy jumps on the back of the robot and they start to take off.

Squealer yelled, "Hey stop—that's not yours!" He ran over to the edge of the loading dock and jumped off onto the pavement.

Stacy screamed, "Stop them, Squealer, stop them, stop them!"

He picked up a gallon of ice cream and chucked it at the boy and his robot, hitting the boy in the arm, jerking the handlebars that were attached to the robot on wheels. The boy and his robot skidded into a telephone pole and wrecked. Before they could do anything, Squealer ran over there and pinned the boy down, yelling for Stacy to call the police.

The police came and took the boy away—a tow truck picked up the robot.

Adam Iler

"Anything else I can do for ya?" Squealer asked Stacy.

"How 'bout them boxes?" Stacy smiled.

"Your wish is my command, my lady," Squealer bowed.

Stacy curtsied. "Perhaps, my lord will take another bowl of cheetah dots as reward?"

"You bet!"

As Squealer was finishing up yet another bowl of cheetah dots, an orange light through the plate glass window startled him. "What's that orange light outside the store?"

"Silly pig, that's the sun going down!"

"That's the sun going down?!?" Squealer repeated. "I have to go!" Squealer said.

"Ok—well, thanks for all your help today!"

"Sure thing, Stacy. Be seeing ya!"

Squealer ran out of the door, almost running over a couple coming in. "Sorry, folks, sorry." He took off running again, and as he did, Squealer could hear the woman saying to the man, "Isn't that the pig who saved the town from the robot?" He replied, "I think you're right, dear."

Squealer got to his scooter and took off down the road to get back to his house. People in cars waved to him. One passenger slammed a newspaper up against the car window; it had a picture of Squealer waving with the robot behind him. Squealer pointed at the picture, then gave a big thumbs up.

He turned down the alleyway and pulled up to his hidden door. He looked around to see if the coast was clear, then picked up the garbage can and started heading over to the other side of the door. He was just about to set the garbage can down when he felt a tug on his shirt. This startled him and he almost threw the can down the alleyway. Squealer flung around to see what was pulling on him.

There in front of him stood a bright, green-eyed, sandy-brown, blond-haired boy. "Hey there, Mr. Pig-Pig, whatchya doing?"

Squealer scratched his head and looked around, then looked back down. "Where are your mommy and daddy?" Squealer asked.

"I'm not sure," he said, looking around and then back up at Squealer. He had tears in his eyes and his bottom lip starting to shake.

Squealer bent down on one knee and said, "I'll help you find them."

Squealer could hear someone calling, "Tyler, Tyler." Squealer looked up. There was a woman running down the alleyway. Squealer stood up, in case she was going to try hitting him.

She ran up to Squealer and her little boy. She looked at Squealer, then looked down at the little boy and snatched him up. They hugged. The little boy said, "Mommy, I was scared."

She said, "Yah, baby, I was too." They pulled apart with her still holding him. She looked him in the eyes. "You can't run off like that, you understand?"

"Yes." The little boy threw his arms around her again, then in a little voice he said, "Sorry, Mommy."

Squealer just stood there. The mother opened her eyes and looked at Squealer. "Oh, I'm sorry. Thank you very much."

"Not a problem, ma'm. He just came up behind me—he scared me more then I scared him." The woman looked at Squealer again and stepped back. "Wait a second—aren't you that pig who's going around town and stopping all those weird robots?"

Squealer rubbed the back of his neck. "Yah, that's me."

"You are doing such a great job. Just let me say that we need someone like you around here."

Squealer was getting a little shy. "Thanks a lot, ma'm."

She looked back at her little boy. "And I can't wait to tell your daddy about this one. The little boy smiled. "Thank you again, Squealer. You don't know how much I appreciate you doing this and the rest of the town does too. If there's anything I can ever do for you, just let me know." As the mother and boy walked away, Squealer yelled after them, "There are harnesses that are made for toddlers now!" The woman just shook her head. The little boy waved back at Squealer, and said, "Bye-bye, Mr. Pig-Pig. Squealer waved back and mumbled to himself, "Bye- bye, little rug rat."

Whack a Mole

S quealer waited until they left the alleyway before he put the garbage can on the spot to lift the door up. He looked up. The sun had a few more minutes before it set, so he went into his secret lair. He told his computer to tell him if he had any messages. There was one from the Chief, who was wondering where he was because he needed to be up at the old abandoned mine shaft. Squealer hurried up and jumped into his backpack engage booth, got back on his scooter, and took off towards the mine shaft.

While he was headed up there, it started to rain. He could barely see out of his goggles, so he thought of a hand to wipe the rain off so he could see out of the goggles.

Once he got to the mine shaft, the Chief popped up on Squealer's scooter VisCom.

"It took you long enough to get up there."

"It's a long story, Chief."

The Chief just looked at him. "Yah, I heard that one before. I can't wait to hear it, but here's the deal. Our meter is picking up a lot of movement when it rains up there. The tremors seem to follow the rain clouds down the mountain, but the rain stops before it hits the town of Grumbles Ville."

After the Chief spoke, Squealer's VisCom started going in and out, so he was only picking up bits and pieces what the chief was actually saying. "Chief, come in." Squealer started hitting it on its side. "Stupid thing." Then the VisCom went dead all together.

Great! Now how am I gonna know what this thing even looks like? He started looking around. The rain had slowed down. The ground was wet and the frogs came out and started croaking. Squealer couldn't see anything, so he thought of a big fluid light. He sat down on top of a rock and just listened; within a couple of minutes, a little tremor started—after that one another one—then another, but nothing else would happen.

Squealer climbed off of the rock and started walking around. Suddenly, a big tremor shook the ground so much that branches from trees fell, then trees toppled over. He had to jump out of the way from being smashed by one of the trees that fell, landing face first in dirt.

While Squealer was still on the ground, the dirt underneath him started mounding up a molehill, then it cracked open. Squealer jumped off before he fell into the crack. He looked around to see if anything was coming at him. Then the cracks spread longer and wider. All Squealer could do is run away so he didn't fall into the glowing green cracks.

He began to hear a screeching sound. It got louder and louder behind him, so Squealer turned around to see what it was. While he was backing up, he tripped over a root sticking out of the ground. Landing on the ground again, he let out a little girly scream, then he looked up.

Crawling out of the crack was a giant hairless mole rat. This monster mole rat was barring its teeth, like it wanted to rip into Squealer. The monster mole walked up to him so close that when it let out a scream, Squealer's head was almost inside its mouth.

A long stream of drool came off of one of the mole rat's teeth straight on the top of Squealer's head. Squealer freaked out when he felt that drool and jumped back. He shook his finger at the mole rat. "What's wrong with you?" You don't drool on people," Squealer yelled out.

The mole rat closed his mouth and tilted his head. Then he stuck his nose right into Squealer's belly and started pushing him back. Squealer was now getting mad, so he raised his hand above his head and smacked the mole rat on the nose.

The mole rat rubbed his nose with his claws, and then it stood quietly. Squealer was puzzled. He threw his arms out in front of him with palms up and said, "Are you just gonna stand there, you hairless poo?"

The mole took a run at him.

Squealer pulled his blaster out and fired a shot. The mole

rat turned and ran past him. It turned around and charged Squealer again—and the giant mole rat ran past him.

Squealer reached out and grabbed one of the mole rat's big teeth and hung onto it; the mole rat thrashed his head back and forth. Then the mole rat threw his head back. Squealer flew up into the air and right onto the back of the giant hairless mole rat.

Squealer thought, What do I do now? The mole rat was running around and knocking into trees and bushes, trying to get Squealer off of his back. It was trying so hard to get him off that it slipped into one of the big cracks. The light from the cracks was a very bright green and the closer you got to the light the brighter it got.

Squealer kept getting hit in the face. It wasn't a light tap—it was a hit that would snap back his head. *Whack... Whack.*

He put his hand up in front of his face trying to stop the

pain. Eventually, Squealer was able to grab something in his hand. He struggled to open one of his eyes to see what was smacking him in the face; in his hand was a piece of corn cob. It seems to have a strange greenish glow about it.

Squealer's eyes got really big while corn cobs were hitting him in the forehead. *These pieces of corn cob must be some of the ones missing from the farm, he thought. But why the glow?*

The giant naked mole was burrowing a hole right through the corn cobs, its big, sharp claws cutting the cobs like butter. Squealer couldn't move off the back of the mole because the tunnel was so narrow. Suddenly, there was a huge bang, then a lot of smoke. The blast landed the pig on a pile of corn. Squealer climbed out of the hole, waving his arms to clear the smoke. He looked over at a tree—impaled on a branch was the hairless mole rat. Steam seemed to be rising from the wound. Then Squealer looked around some more; all around the hole were corn cobs lying on the ground when the mole busted out of the tunnel.

Squealer called the Chief on the VisCom, who popped up on the screen reading the evening newspaper (*Things That Slither in the Night*). The Chief looked up nonchalantly. Seeing Squealer on his VisCom, he slammed the paper down on the desk and rubbed his hands down his face. "Sorry, Squealer, just seeing what's in the news."

"Chief, I think I found all the missing corn."

The Chief leaned into the VisCom and tilted his head. "Was it a ghost? The Giant Buffalo Worm? I know—it was the Spike-Furred Woodland Beast!"

"No…no…" Squealer shouted, "it was a giant hairless mole rat!"

The Chief threw up his arms, then pushed himself back into the chair. "Of course! The giant hairless mole rat! Why didn't I think of that?"

"You know about the giant hairless mole rat?" Squealer asked.

"Ah, nope, I don't think I have. I heard about a man beaver, a duck monkey—how about a cat millipede...?" and the Chief just kept going on and on until Squealer had to step in. "Chief, you're scaring me."

"Hey, when you've seen as many creepy things as I have, you become creepy yourself." Squealer got a quizzical look on his face "O-o-o...k."

The Chief asked, "Where's that giant hairless mole rat at?"

Squealer grabbed the camera and turned it around to reveal the mole impaled on the twisted tree. "There he is, Chief. He's not doing too good right now."

The Chief's eyes got really big. "What's that—steam coming out of the wound? Could it be a biomechanical mole rat?"

"Gee, I don't know, Chief. I do know that the corn cobs seem to have a green glow about them."

"Green glow, you say? I don't like that—I don't like that one bit. They may be full of radiation."

"But isn't that dangerous, Chief, radiation? I mean, I was surrounded by the stuff."

"Don't worry about it, boy, your backpack automatically protects you from that sort of danger."

"Whew—good to know, Chief."

"Now, I've got to get that big guy out of there." He hit a button on his console and ordered his guys to the scene. Squealer started to say something when he heard something off in the distance.

He looked around but couldn't see anything. It kept getting louder and louder, but he still couldn't see where the noise was coming from. Suddenly a spotlight right above Squealer hit him. Squealer got scared and tried to escape the light, but he couldn't outrun it.

He got up enough courage to finally look up to see what it was. Squealer saw a couple of guys repelling down ropes from a helicopter. They ran over to Squealer and told him that they would be taking the mole rat off of his hands.

He just shrugged his shoulders and said, "Ok."

The men hooked a huge claw around the giant hairless mole rat. Then each of them grabbed onto repelling rope to be pulleyed back up into the helicopter. The claw, connected to the chopper, lifted the mole off the ground and carried it away.

They left Squealer standing there looking at the helicopter getting smaller and smaller in the distance.

Roller's Lair

Squealer kicked a rock, then started walking through the bushes and leaves. He was very confused about what just happened.

He found a pathway that he started walking along; the path had a few twists and turns, ending at the side of a mountain. Squealer thought, *This is kinda odd.* He looked around for a clue, but his belly began rumbling so loud that he almost shook the ground. He rubbed his belly, then looked around some more.

Squealer spotted some of those wild spore berries that he loved to munch on, so he grabbed some and tossed them down his bottomless pit. After filling his belly, he managed to pull himself up to his feet and stumbled over to the mountainside. Squealer rubbed the side of the mountain like it would tell him a secret. He heard some noises in the bushes. Squealer turned around—two chasers.

Squealer tried to grab his ray gun but he couldn't get it out in time. One of the chasers launched a net over him and the other shot a dart at Squealer. His eyes got heavy and he started to see double—then it went dark.

Squealer woke up hanging in a glass cage with two holes

in each side and two metal skulls framing each hole. It was hanging over a pot of boiling liquid. As he came round, he heard a distant voice say, "Wakey wakey, eggs an bacy. Wake up, you good for nothing pig...You fat little pig...Always getting in the way, always making my oil boil. But now I'm gonna get rid of my problem."

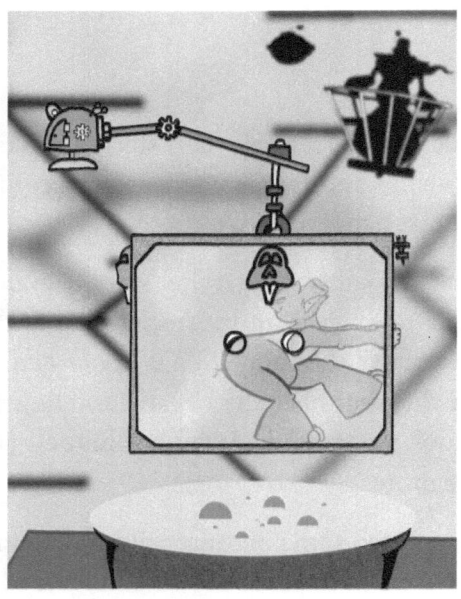

Squealer looked down at him, then asked, "Is your little problem a new oil change?"

Roller flew one of his hovercrafts up to the cage that Squealer was in. "Look at me, you little stupid, stupid pig!"

Squealer looked at Roller. "Why are you so angry?"

Roller threw up his arms. "I'm angry because nobody seriously believes I'm taking over this lame planet!"

Roller shook his head.

Adam Iler

"No, no—Why am I telling you this? I should be dipping you in that boiling pot down there. With you out of the way, I can take over the planet, then start my master plan—and this is the point that I'll shut up now." Roller flew back down on his hovercraft.

Squealer sat down and asked with a grin, "Can't you fill me in on your master plan?"

Roller spun back around, then let out a sinister laugh. "My plan is so evil that I will not just take over this pathetic planet but all the other ones with it.

Squealer reached an arm through the hole that was cut out in the glass of the cage and pointed a finger at Roller. "You won't get away with this one, Roller!" When he pulled back his arm, Squealer slammed his hand against the glass—not just one time but twice. He finally got his hand back in, then rubbed it to ease the pain.

Roller shook his head and chuckled. "This is gonna be easier than I thought." Then he flew away. Squealer knew that he had to get out and stop Roller. *With my backpack nothing can stop me—say, wait a minute—where's my backpack? It definitely isn't on me. Dang, Roller must've taken it.*

He went over to the locked cage door and thumped his forehead with his fist. "Think, Squealer, think…" He tried pulling the lock off, then he tried kicking the door open with his big round foot. Nothing.

Getting tired, Squealer leaned against one side of the cage and took a breather. Suddenly he felt something poking at his back through one of the holes. He turned around. Outside the cage was a little robot, slender and round like a smashed pop can.

Squealer looked around. "Can I help you?"

The little robot just stared at him, then spoke up. "I should ask you the same thing. I think I can help you."

"Why would you help me? You work for Roller, don't you?"

"Yes, he works me all the time."

"Yes, Roller never turns us off. He's all about making those stupid chasers. Roller's got thousands of these sharp-toothed bread boxes waiting for his word to attack. I just had to get out of there; I'm not going to be like those old robots on the line, that rust and fall apart making those things."

The little robot looked at him, then said, "You do want to get out of here, don't you?"

Squealer nodded his head. "Of course I do. Whatever Roller's up to, I have to stop him before he hurts anyone else."

With the helicopter blades on top of his head, the little robot flew over to the door, of the cage. "Stand back and cover your eyes."

Squealer flattened himself against the opposite side of cage, then turned his head and covered his eyes.

Two wires came out of the side of the robot's body. He touched them together. One of them sparked with a bit of smoke, then he put it against the lock on the door and it blew right off. The little robot was thrown into a metal pole. Squealer went to the door then kicked it off the hinges.

The little robot flew over to him. Squealer looked at the robot. "I don't know what to say, but thanks. Do you have a name?"

The little robot said, "T-cup."

Squealer just looked at T-cup and said, "Ok."

Squealer began to climb down when T-cup wrapped his wire hand around his arm. "Hold on there, Squealer, can you take me with you?"

"Take you with me, T-cup? I don't even know where I'm going."

"I don't want to be here anymore, especially around that lunatic Roller. Please take me with you—please..."

Squealer thought about it for a bit, then shrugged. "Sure, why not? You can help find my backpack, which is lost."

T-cup asked, "What's so special about this item?"

"Well, it's attached to my blast gun; it's got lot of power and it gives me tools to use."

T-cup responded, "Just like Roller's?"

Squealer's eyes got big. "What did you say, T-cup? Roller has a powered backpack?"

"Sure, he's had it for a very long time. He never shows anyone."

"Let's go find my backpack!" Squealer grabbed the bottom of the cage and swung underneath but he forgot one little thing—that he was a very fat pig who can't hold his own weight, so Squealer fell like a ton of bricks down to the floor made of metal grating.

T-cup flew down to Squealer as he was brushing himself off. "What were you thinking?"

"What are you talking about, T-cup? I slipped."

"Yeah, right…"

Squealer and T-cup took off through the maze of metal grates. They heard some noise around one of the corners, so they peeked around. Around the corner there was one of Roller's chasers, but this one was beefed up three times as big and made of thicker metal.

The chaser started flashing and vibrating, then turned towards them and charged, knocking Squealer onto a lower level platform of this multi-level maze. T-cup could see this wasn't going to come out too good and flew over to Squealer. He wrapped his wires around his arms and pulled him up, but it wasn't easy. The two of them kept going up and down as sparks shot out of the top of T-cup's helicopter blades on the top of his head.

Squealer started screaming because they were just a few feet above the boiling liquid. "I'm smelling ham and I think I know where its coming from!"

Adam Iler

T-cup blurted out, "Don't make me laugh—I'm trying to save you!"

T-cup pulled with all his might to get them to a very high platform. When they reached it, T-cup couldn't hold on to Squealer anymore and let go. They both fell hard on the metal grating. Squealer ran over to T-cup, who was just laying there with sparks shooting out of his shell. Squealer picked him up. "Hey, there, come back—follow the smell of ham."

T-cup started making noises. Squealer put him down on the metal grate and then stood up over T-cup. A bright light shot out of the robot. Squealer had to turn his head because the light was getting too intense. Then he heard somebody say, "Squealer." He turned around and there in his face was T-cup. It startled Squealer, who screamed and backed up, falling right off the metal grate and landing on his back onto a lower one.

T-cup flew over to the edge of the metal grate, then yelled out, "Squealer!"

The pig yelled back, "O-o-u-u-c-h!" It took a while for him to get up. "We have to find my power backpack."

They both looked around. On one of the platforms was a metal box with two of the big reinforced chasers guarding it. Squealer asked, "What are we going to do, T-cup? Those are some mean chasers. You saw what one of their kind did to me."

"How could I forget?"

"I'm glad we lost that first one." Squealer started walking down the walkway. "Follow me, T-cup."

"Where are you going?"

"I'm going to get my backpack and stop that Roller once and for all."

T-cup flew up behind Squealer then asked, "How are we going to get the backpack, Squealer?"

"I'm not sure yet."

T-cup and Squealer crawled onto the metal platform below. Squealer looked up at the metal chasers. They kept going around and around the box. T-cup looked at Squealer and put his wire arms up to say, "what now?" Squealer looked back at him and just shrugged his shoulders.

T-cup flew off up towards the bottom of the box. Squealer threw his arms in the air, then mouthed, "What are you doing?"

He flew right beneath the metal box, then stuck his wire arm up to the bottom. Sparks shot out of his wire arm and then he started cutting out the bottom of the metal box. Squealer began dancing around and watching the progress of T-cup cutting.

T-cup looked down at Squealer to see what he was doing when he noticed that one of the big guard chasers was watching him. T-cup flew away. The chaser started flashing. T-cup flew up to the chaser, turned his flame on, and went for his sensor eye. The chaser backed away from T-cup, then a little panel opened up on the chaser and three missiles came out then without any warning. They shot out but they couldn't lock on T-cup and flew right by him with force.

By now the chaser was close enough for Squealer to grab, so he jumped up off the platform he was on (a whole two inches) and grabbed onto the metal chaser. With all of his might, he slammed the chaser down on the grate then crushed it in.

Squealer looked up at T-cup and started to laugh. T-cup flew down towards Squealer, and Squealer picked up the chaser and showed its backside to T-cup, which had indentations from the grate. T-cup said, "I'm impressed."

Squealer said, "Great job, T-cup."

"Thanks. I just thought, 'metal and fire don't mix and I have both of them.'" Then T-cup saw that Squealer's eyes were getting big and he was backing up. "What's wrong?"

What the two had forgotten was that there were two chasers guarding the metal box.

Squealer yelled, "Watch out, T-cup!"

The little robot turned around. Flying straight at him was the other guard chaser with two sets of missiles coming out of its sides.

The chaser flew right by T-cup and straight at Squealer. He jumped out of the way from being hit by the chaser. T-cup shot a flame, but it didn't faze it—the chaser wanted Squealer.

By this time T-cup had cut a line around the whole

bottom of the box except for one of the corners. Squealer jumped at the chaser and landed on top of him, then jumped off the chaser toward the corner of the box and grabbed onto the metal that was still connected and just hung there. T-cup yelled out, "Hey, this is no time to be hanging around."

Squealer couldn't believe that the metal piece didn't fall with all his weight on it, so he started bouncing to break the corner off. Finally, the piece started to bend and finally snapped. He went down and the bottom of the metal box went down right on top of him; Squealer laid there for a moment, then pushed the metal off of him. There, three feet away from him, was his power backpack. He rolled himself over to it and grabbed the ray gun and held down the trigger to increase the power of the ray, then opened fire at the chaser.

The chaser blew up in a bright fireball, with metal pieces flying everywhere.

T-cup flew over to Squealer. "That was about the coolest thing that I have ever seen in my life—and my life hasn't been that long!"

Squealer had his backpack in his hands trying to figure out how to get it on without his backpack machine. "This is going to be a problem, T-cup."

"Let me see it," T-cup said, so Squealer handed it over to him. "Turn around, this might sting." T-cup put one of his wire arms into the backpack and shoved his other arm into Squealer's back. Squealer dropped to his knees and started screaming—and then the pain stopped. Squealer stood up and felt the backpack on his back. When he realized what T-cup did for him, Squealer started dancing around—and then when he started thinking about how T-cup did it he yelled out, *"That's gross!"*

He took off running down the metal walkway and said, "Here I come, Roller."

Roller must have heard Squealer, because chasers started coming at him from every direction. He kneeled on one knee, pulled out his ray gun, and started blasting away. There were chaser carcasses scattered all over, but the chasers kept on coming. There was no stopping them. Squealer knew that he had to get up and get to somewhere else, so he stood up and started walking down the platform. He just kept picking them off one by one.

Squealer saw where the chasers were coming from, so in between picking them off one by one he started firing at the round door that they kept coming out of. He had to shoot the open door's frame a few times before it got red hot and exploded. Shards of metal went flying everywhere and it almost hit our fearless hero in the belly. All he could think of was the big dinner that he had eaten the night before—what a waste it would've been if that piece of metal had cut his belly open and it spilt out onto the floor.

Squealer leaped onto the platform to the door that blew up; he peeked his head in. On the other side was a machine room that Roller built all of the chasers in. Squealer quietly stepped in and looked around. There were robotic arms that were carrying metal parts and others that were welding parts onto other parts along the assembly line.

Squealer found himself down by the assembly line watching the robotic arms welding some of the parts together for the super chaser; he heard a loud noise, like somebody getting onto a speaker.

It was Roller. "Well, well…attention all the fat little pigs out there—and that means you, Squealer. I'm impressed that you made it this far, but I'm sorry that you will not be making it any further, because I'm going to have to hurt you very badly and put your head up on a wall, if that's Ok with you. I actually feel somewhat sorry for you."

Squealer yelled out, "Why? I'll be feeling sorry for *you*, stupid robot, when I get through with you. Or maybe you'd like the Chief to change your evil computer chip to a normal one!"

Roller snickered. "Oh really? I'm going to introduce you to my greatest creation—meet SF ROB."

Squealer laughed. "What the heck is that, you cracked robot?"

Roller got frustrated and spit out, "It means 'smash and flatten robot.'"

Squealer replied, "Oh, Ok, that's nice. I'll be seeing you now." He then turned and tried to walk away while saying, "Smash…Flatten…"

That's when something came busting through one of the walls. Squealer couldn't see what it was until the dust cleared. Standing in front of him was a huge robot—but that wasn't the weird part. Squealer looked closer and there in the center of the robot's chest was Flip-Flop, Squealer's Betta, inside his fish bowl.

"How could you?" Squealer yelled out."

Flip-Flop got on his voice amplifier. "You try to spend your life in a little bowl. At least Roller feeds me the good fish food and not that crappy food that you give me."

SF ROB hovered off the platform and right in front of Squealer. It stood in front of him like a building. Roller screamed out, "What are you waiting for? Crush him!"

Flip-Flop looked up at the loudspeaker. "That's one of the other machines that you built for me, Roller. I'm in the Smash and Flatten robot right now, as you well know."

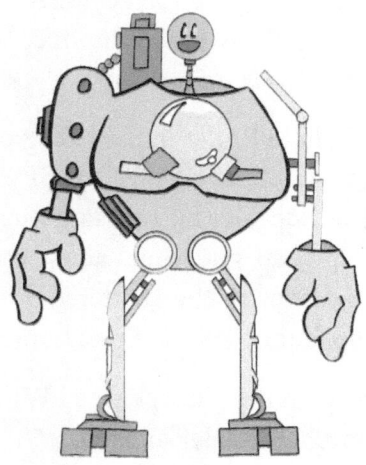

"Would you just get him, or I'll cut you off from the project."

"O-k…"

So Flip-Flop started pulling levers and pushing buttons. The SF ROB lifted his arms in the air and thrust them down in a hammer throw right at Squealer, who rolled out of the way, then started to bob and weave so he wouldn't get hit. He grabbed his ray gun.

"Ok, Flip-Flop, let's dance."

"How about this?" Flip-Flop wound up pulling a lever and all the metal on the SF ROB got thicker and stronger. Squealer's jaw just dropped and his arms fell to his sides.

Squealer ran around trying to find a weak spot on the SF ROB. After awhile he just slapped himself on the forehead and said to himself, *Good job, Roller, on making this robot.* Flip-Flop shot a hurt ball at Squealer; a hurt ball is a cannonball that has spikes on it and is attached to a chain. The ball flew straight at him and he covered his eyes. All Squealer heard was a thud; he opened his eyes. The hurt ball was on the ground being wound back up.

Squealer could here Roller in the background screaming at Flip-Flop to get rid of the fat pig. The SF ROB wound up grabbing a hold of Squealer and tossing him through a big glass window. Flip-Flop got a menacing grin on his face. The robot hovered over to the shattered window. Squealer struggled to get up, but he couldn't pull himself to his feet.

Roller spoke up on the loudspeaker. "What's wrong, pig? Can't fight anymore?" Squealer screamed, "At least I can fight my own battles, Roller."

"Not for long," Roller said.

Squealer stumbled to his feet and said, "Let's do this." He ran up to the SF ROB and grabbed onto the bottom of his foot, trying to flip it. Flip-Flop pushed a button and the robot raised its hand as high as it could. It swung it down with all its force right on top of Squealer's head. He fell on his butt and saw nothing but birds and stars.

Then the SF ROB grabbed Squealer by the foot and then started swinging him above its head, flung him into the air, and then shot out the hurt ball. *Smack...*

Squealer hit the metal grate and slid across it into the wall. He lay there for awhile, trying to catch his breath. Roller laughed out loud and commanded, "Flip-Flop, finish him."

"Your wish is my command."

Squealer crawled to his knees; his right eye was swelling shut with a couple of cuts here and there. Parts of his power backpack was falling off as he rose up.

Squealer grabbed his ray gun and held down the trigger until it was fully powered, then looked up at Flip-Flop. "Sorry, my friend, but I have to do this." Squealer pointed his ray gun at Flip-Flop's bowl and shot the power ray. The power ray went right threw the Betta's fish bowl and right out the robot's back.

The FS ROB fell to its knees and dropped. Squealer lowered his head, in mourning.

He stumbled to his feet and looked over to the broken, empty fish bowl. Squealer took a deep breath, then tilted his head back and screamed, shaking his fist, "Roller, you coward! Show yourself right now! I got rid of your robot and one of my so-called best friends. Fight your own battle, Roller."

"Stupid, stupid pig.... I have no problem destroying you so I can get rid of you once and for all. This world is mine once you are out of the picture."

Squealer yelled out, "No more talking, Roller. Time to settle this once and for all."

"Silly pig, if you want a fight, then that's what I'll give you."

Squealer stood there looking around, waiting for Roller or any one of his menacing robots to start moving toward him. He heard a whirling sound, but he couldn't figure out where it was coming from. Squealer planted his feet firmly and gripped his ray gun tighter. All of a sudden, Roller came up underneath the metal floor on a moving platform.

He had a smug look on his face. "Here I am, pig. "This is what you wanted, right?" Squealer took a running leap and jumped on his back. Roller started yelling, "What are you doing? Get off me...."

"No way!"

Roller pushed buttons on his armband, then Squealer saw some chasers coming their way. "Get them away from us, Roller, right now."

"Why should I, pig?"

"I'll start pulling out wires," he told Roller.

"You wouldn't dare, fat piggy." Squealer popped one of Roller's circuit panels out. Roller started rolling away from the chasers with Squealer still on his back. The robot started crying out, "Get away from us, you stupid little chasers, before he does something to me!"

The chasers disappeared one by one; Squealer jumped off Roller's back, then got his ray gun out and walked around to the front of him. "Don't you move, Roller, or I won't hesitate blasting you with my ray gun!"

"Come on, little brave piggy, you are so heroic." Then Roller said, "Squealer" and when he said it he acted like he threw up some oil in his mouth. "Can't we work out something, pig? I have a lot of scrap metal that I can give you so you can move from that small farm to a bigger one."

Squealer screamed out, "I don't live on a farm."

Roller looked surprised.

"Yeah, I live in an apartment," Squealer mumbled.

"And where is this apartment at?"

"Well, it's above—hey, wait a second."

While he had his guard down, one of the super chasers ran straight into the side of Squealer and knocked him down. He tried to get up but he couldn't, so Squealer pulled himself toward Roller, who was getting away. Then he passed out.

Roller, on the other hand, rolled himself to his command center and locked himself inside with his many locks on his thick metal door. "That stupid little pig, he'll never get in here."

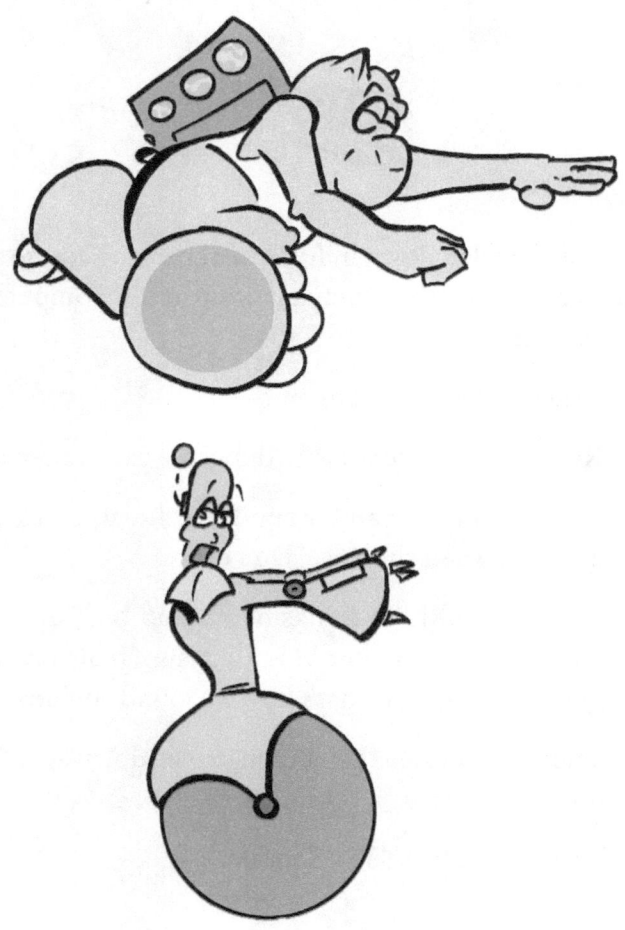

Chief kneeled down in front of Squealer. "You see, when you started with this company you had a computer chip imbedded in you."

"When did you put it in me?"

"Remember all those awful things we gave you to drink?"

Squealer put his hand around his throat, stuck out his tongue, and started choking. "Do I ever!"

"Well, one of those drinks had a chip that, once drank, will imbed itself into your blood stream. That way, we can track your movements. That's how we found you down here."

Squealer rubbed his belly, then looked down at it. "There's a computer chip floating around in there somewhere?"

The Chief sighed. "Yes, Squealer."

One of the Chief's men helped the pig up. As soon as he stood up, he yelled, "Roller!"

"What about Roller?" the Chief asked. "Squealer, we looked all over this labyrinth of cages; we weren't able to find that crazy robot."

"So what now?"

The Chief crossed his arms and rubbed his chin. Well, it's time to move onto your next case, Squealer."

"I didn't catch that mean Roller, though."

The Chief said, "I think it won't be the last time you're going to see that strange robot."

"I guess you're right, and when you're right, you're right, and you're right, Chief.

The Chief just looked at him.

"Ok, Ok, I get the hint," Squealer said.

When Squealer began walking away, one of the agents opened one of the doors and hundreds of thousands of corn cobs came pouring out. "You might want to take a look at this Chief."

The Chief walked over to the door and looked into the room. He then turned around and said, "Nice job, Squealer, it seems you found the bottom of the mystery of the missing corn."

Squealer just smiled...

That's where this story ends before Squealer goes on to another adventure. Tune in on the next adventure to see what our hero gets himself into next.